INDESTRUCTIBLES®

For ages 0 and up!

BOOKS BABIES CAN REALLY SINK THEIR GUMS INTO!

Where is the horse? Running in the field!

Where are the chickens? Playing with their chicks!

Where are the sheep? Frolicking in the grass!

Dear Parents: INDESTRUCTIBLES are built for the way babies "read": with their hands and mouths. INDESTRUCTIBLES won't rip or tear and are 100% washable. They're made for baby to hold, grab, chew, pull, and bend.

CHEW ALL THESE AND MORE!

$5.95 US ISBN 978-0-7611-5698-7
50595
9 780761 156987

Library of Congress Cataloging-in-Publication Data is available.
WORKMAN is a registered trademark of Workman Publishing Co., Inc.
First printing October 2009
2 0 19 18 17 16 15

All INDESTRUCTIBLES books have been safety-tested and meet or exceed ASTM-F963 and CPSIA guidelines.

Contact specialmarkets@workman.com regarding special discounts for bulk purchases.
Printed in China

WORKMAN PUBLISHING CO., INC. 225 Varick Street, New York, NY 10014 • indestructiblesinc.com